STAY!

Alex Latimer

PEACHTREE
ATLANTA

Olive & Columbo

Thanks for the inspiration.

Ω

Published by
PEACHTREE PUBLISHERS
1700 Chattahoochee Avenue
Atlanta, Georgia 30318-2112
www.peachtree-online.com

Text and Illustrations © 2015 by Alex Latimer

First published in Great Britain in 2015 by Picture Corgi, an imprint of
Random House Children's Books. First United States version
published in 2015 by Peachtree Publishers.

The illustrations were created as pencil drawings, digitized, then finished with color and texture.

Printed in April 2015 in China
10 9 8 7 6 5 4 3 2 1
First Edition

ISBN 978-1-56145-884-4

Cataloging-in-Publication Data is available from the Library of Congress

best in show

Ben thought his dog Buster was
the best dog in the whole world,

but Mum and Dad were not so sure.

BUSTER!

Buster was EXHAUSTING!

"I think we need a vacation!"

"Vacation!"
Ben couldn't wait.

Until he remembered
the last trip...

"Buster will stay with Grampa!" said Mum and Dad firmly.

"But Grampa doesn't know all the things that Buster likes to do," argued Ben.

"Then why don't you tell Grampa in a note?" asked Dad.

Ben found some paper and his pencils and crayons, and started to write…

After he had written his note,
Ben took Buster for a walk.

And after that, he wrote another note.

Don't let Buster off the leash if you see any of the following...

In fact, the more Ben thought about it,
the more notes he needed to write …

A few things for Buster:

Dad's slipper, so he doesn't chew yours

My teddy

Dog biscuits (2 if he's been good, only 1 if he's been bad)

His leash for walks

Food bowl. Stand back wh he eats - it a c t

_ those Buster's paw prints?

Yes, that's him

No - a bird

No - neighbor's cat

No - Dad

orite Season

umn is

for squi

When should Buster have a bath?

② When he's changed color (Unless he's green - then go straight to the vet.)

☐ good
☑ OK
☐ bad

① Your eyes sting when you pet him

③ Before Aunt Agnes visits

④ When he's had a long day

How many time

bark

One bark is ok

Ten

bark bark bark

So

Twi

And by the time the family was ready to set off, Ben had more notes than he could count.

"I feel like I've forgotten something important," Ben said.

"Well, you can always send it to me on a postcard," replied Grampa. "Now have a great time!"

Ben hugged Buster goodbye (careful not to squeeze too tightly).

Ben did have a great time, but he kept remembering
things that he'd forgotten to tell Grampa.
So he wrote them all down
on postcards.

barking at in the middle of the night?

funny noises

nothing

Post Card

For Correspondence — Address Only

Things Buster shouldn't eat:

egg shells

candy wrappers

chocolate

compost

furniture

peanut butter from the jar

What's Buster dreaming of?

chasing squirrels (Don't wake him, he'll be sad.)

tongue out means he's dreaming about dinner

Where does Buster

water bowl

fish pond

Toilet

But he was still
sure he'd forgotten
something important …

When Mum felt sick after eating a bad hot dog, it reminded Ben of something to tell Grampa.

Diagnosis Chart
(What's wrong with Buster?)

sunburn

lovesick

x-ray

ate a toy dinosaur

just needs to pee

And when Dad took a wrong turn on the way to see a famous waterfall, Ben wrote another note.

If Buster gets lost, where will he be?

POSTALE.   POSTKARTE.

(FOR ADDRESS ONLY.)

waiting outside school

sleeping under a tree

Knocking over garbage cans

chasing deer in the woods

chasing the mailman

But it was only then that he remembered the very important thing he'd forgotten—and he wrote one last note as quickly as he could.

IMPORTANT!

Never take Buster
to the post office!
He knows that's
where mailmen
come from.
Love, Ben

danger!

But the note arrived too late. Grampa and Buster were already on their way to the post office to pick up a package.

Buster was banned from the post office! And Grampa thought that perhaps it was time to cure the dog of his bad behavior.

So he began to train Buster.

I have a bone for you if you listen.

It was hard work.

Very hard work.

But Grampa knew that hard work always pays off in the end.

When Ben arrived home, Grampa had
a note of his own ready for him.

...missing you.

Ben couldn't help it—he hugged Grampa
and Buster as hard as he could.

In the weeks that followed, Grampa gave Ben
a few extra notes about how to train Buster.

And they worked so well
that Mum even said Buster
could come along on the
next family vacation.

This time he didn't bark (or fart) in the car.

And he didn't chase any birds at all.

He was a very well-behaved dog...